EEYORE,
You're the Best!

By Ann Braybrooks
Illustrated by John Kurtz

A GOLDEN BOOK • NEW YORK

Golden Books Publishing Company, Inc., Racine, Wisconsin 53404

Library of Congress Catalog Card Number: 95-77694 ISBN: 0-307-98765-5
MCMXCVII

One morning in spring, when the birds were chirping and the daisies were smiling everywhere, Eeyore woke up with a black cloud hovering over him.

"It's the only cloud in the sky," Eeyore groaned, "and it's drizzling. Right on me. Somehow I'm not surprised."

Eeyore lived in a gloomy place and he was rather fond of gray, gloomy things. But this day he had hoped to wake up in a sunnier mood. It was talent show day in the Hundred-Acre Wood!

All week Eeyore had been practicing to show off his somersaults. Now it looked as if this cloud would get in the way. How could a donkey turn somersaults if he was wet?

Eeyore thought he would try to shake the cloud off. He stepped to the right. The cloud moved right with him.

So he jumped to the left, with a bit of a twist. Again the cloud scooted after him.

"Oh, well," said the sad, soggy donkey. "Can't be in the talent show with this thing following me. Better go tell everyone."

Eeyore dragged himself and his cloud off to Christopher Robin's, where the talent show was just getting under way.

Onstage, Pooh was juggling two apples while balancing a stack of honey pots on his head. Christopher Robin, the judge, was busy taking notes.

Eeyore didn't want to disturb anyone, so he stood in the back, with the cloud still hanging over him and the drizzle still drizzling.

When Pooh had finished, Eeyore tried to get Christopher Robin's attention.

"Ahem," he coughed loudly. "Ahem."

But no one could hear Eeyore over the wild clapping and cheering.

Finally, after the applause ended, Christopher Robin heard Eeyore. "Would you like to go next?" the boy asked kindly.

"Me?" said Eeyore, peering through the drizzle. "I can't."

"Sure you can, Buddy-Boy," Tigger chimed in. "That cloud is part of your act, isn't it?"

Eeyore shook his head. "Nope. I woke up with it. I just came here to say that I won't be in the show."

As Eeyore and his cloud turned to go, Pooh called, "Wait! You can still watch."

"Please stay, Eeyore," cried Roo and Piglet together.

A raindrop slid down Eeyore's nose. "Well . . ." he said.

So, along with the others, Eeyore watched as
Roo played a drum while hopping on one foot.

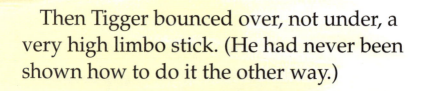

Then Tigger bounced over, not under, a
very high limbo stick. (He had never been
shown how to do it the other way.)

Rabbit sang a lovely song about spring as he tossed carrots and radishes into the audience.

Then Eeyore shifted to a dry spot.
Piglet read from a Very Dramatic Play.

Kanga danced a short ballet.

And Owl recited a poem about his large family tree, beginning with his ancestor Lord Oakley.

Finally it was time to announce the winner. Christopher Robin began, "The ribbon goes to . . . to everyone!" Then he quickly added, "Everyone's act was terrific, so you all win! Winners, please come onstage."

Alone in the back with his cloud and drizzle, Eeyore watched his friends gather around Christopher Robin.

He felt so gloomy that he didn't hear Christopher Robin invite him onstage, too.

Suddenly Pooh cried, "Look, everybody—
a rainbow!"

As Eeyore stood there, wet and gloomy under his cloud, the afternoon sun shone through the drizzle, and a lovely little Eeyore-sized rainbow appeared over his head.

"Hooray for Eeyore!" everyone shouted.

"Eeyore should win!" yelled Roo.

Then Eeyore's friends lifted him onto their shoulders. And Eeyore raised his head and smiled, while drizzle still drizzled and the rainbow glowed in the sunlight.